PIRATE'S BOUNTY

A TIME TRAVEL ADVENTURE

VICTORIA RUSH

VOLUME 1

RILEY'S TIME TRAVEL ADVENTURES - BOOK 1

COPYRIGHT

For the uninhibited...

WANT TO AMP UP YOUR SEX LIFE?

Sign up for my newsletter to receive more free books and other steamy stuff. Discover a hundred different ways to wet your whistle!

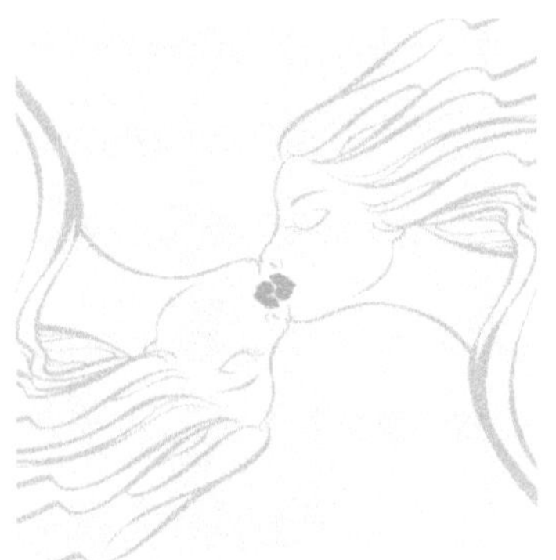

Victoria Rush Erotica

1

_____

Riley Jackson had always been a bit of a geek and a tomboy. She loved nothing more than losing herself in the fantasy world of Lord of the Rings, traveling to faraway lands to experience epic adventures and overcoming heroic odds to defeat a powerful enemy. But now that she'd entered her second year at MIT, the reality of her new life as an engineering student at one of the country's most advanced universities had set in. She'd chosen the quixotic topic of time travel for her undergraduate thesis, and while her physics professor had chided her for choosing such a 'mythical' subject, she was determined to prove him wrong.

One day while walking between classes, she stumbled upon a strange-looking smartphone resting under a bush. After looking around to see if anyone was nearby, she picked up the device and examined it carefully. It was thicker than most of the latest models and had no recognizable manufacturer name. It would have been easy for her to drop it off at the nearest campus lost-and-found depot, but the engineer in her was curious. What was the origin of the mysterious device and why would its owner be so absent-minded to leave it lying in the grass?

She tapped the surface a few times, hoping to find a clue as to its source, but the only thing that appeared on the screen was an empty box for entering a six-digit passcode and an image of a wormhole-like celestial object in the background. Realizing the odds of her decrypting the passcode was a million to one, she considered leaving it where she found it, thinking the owner might retrace his steps to recover it. But she knew it was just as likely someone else would pick it up and keep it as a souvenir. When she returned to her dorm room, she closed the door behind her and sat down at her desk, staring at the passcode box with a blank expression.

How hard could it be to decipher the code? she thought to herself. After all, most people use codes that reflect some aspect of their personal lives. The fact that the phone was left on the campus of MIT meant it likely belonged to another student or professor. Maybe the code had something to do with the university and its surroundings? After unsuccessfully plugging in familiar place names like Barker Dome, Hayden Library, and the Kresge Auditorium, she paused, pinching her eyebrows at the screen.

Could the code have something to do with the cryptic image of the wormhole on the screen? But *wormhole* and *black hole* had too many characters. She knew wormholes were based on Albert Einstein's theory of general relativity, but the words *Einstein* and *Relativity* were also too long. Could it be a simple matter of entering his most famous equation? Riley punched in the formula $E=MC2$, but there was still one field missing. After adding each of the numbers one through nine to the last field, she began to worry that the device would lock up after too many failed attempts.

Then she realized that she'd forgotten to try one final digit – *zero* – and after entering the number, the phone suddenly began to shake violently in her hand. Within seconds, a swirling holographic vortex rose up from the surface, making her hair fly in every direction. Mesmerized by the fascinating light effect, she reached out to touch the edge of the apparition then she felt her body being slowly pulled into the funnel.

"What the...*no!*" she cried, trying to stop herself from being swallowed up by the swirling cyclone.

But it was too late.

Moments later, she was lifted out of her chair and dragged into a paranormal dimension, tumbling through a blindingly bright, ferociously loud portal like an out-of-control freight train. When the noise suddenly stopped, Riley felt her body drop onto the floor of a dank, dark room smelling of pungent vegetables. She squinted her eyes, raising herself up slowly to peer out the barred opening at the top of the entrance door, then she heard the sound of footsteps of someone walking toward the door.

Unsure where she'd landed, she glanced about her, looking for a place to hide. Finding some crates stacked in the corner, she wedged behind the boxes, feeling her body rocking slowly from side to side. Someone placed a key in the lock and when the door opened, a young woman dressed in a pirate costume peered around the storeroom, heading straight toward Riley's direction. When she picked up one of the food crates and noticed Riley hiding in the shadows, she peered at the stranger with a puzzled expression, then she drew her pistol, pointing it threateningly at Riley.

"Who are you?" she demanded.

"I – I'm Riley," Riley stammered. "Riley Jackson."

"How the hell did you get on board our ship and into this locked storeroom?"

"Ship?" Riley said, hardly believing her what she was hearing. "I have no idea how I got here–"

"Well, we'll see what Captain Kate thinks about that," the girl said, pulling Riley up by her t-shirt. "We have a special way of dealing with stowaways..."

2

———

While Riley was marched at gunpoint toward the rear of the ship, the other sailors onboard stared at her strange clothing, leering and shouting what they thought should be done with her. Riley thought it was odd that every one of them was young and female, since she'd never heard of an all-woman pirate ship in her history books. When they reached the stern compartment of the vessel, they stopped in front of a heavy oak door.

Riley's captor tapped on the door softly, and a woman's voice called back.

"What is it?" the woman said.

"We found a stowaway, captain," the guard announced.

"A *what?*" the captain replied, sounding surprised. "Bring her in."

The guard opened the door and pushed her pistol into Riley's back, motioning for her to move toward a large desk surrounded by bay windows overlooking a brilliant turquoise sea. But it was the woman sitting behind the desk that attracted most of Riley's attention. With long black hair, full sensuous lips, and piercing blue eyes, she hardly looked the part of a pirate captain. Wearing a ruffled blouse that clung to her braless breasts like a second skin, Riley couldn't help noticing the outline of her firm nipples denting the fabric. She couldn't have been much more than Riley's age, and as the two women paused to appraise one another, Riley could feel the sexual tension in the room.

"Where did you find her?" the captain said, standing up and walking out from behind her desk, squinting her eyes as she scrutinized Riley's figure in her tight jeans and t-shirt.

"In the storeroom," the guard said.

"I thought we kept it locked?"

"It was. I have no idea how she managed to get inside."

The captain approached Riley more closely, raising her hand to caress the side of her cheekbone.

"Where are you from?" she said. "You're far too *pale* to be from around these parts."

"Boston," Riley said, thinking it best not yet to reveal many more details until she figured out where she was.

"Boston?" the captain said, lifting her eyebrows. "You're a long way from home. How did you get aboard my ship and into our locked storeroom?"

"It's...*complicated*," Riley said, knowing nobody would believe her improbable story that she'd been transported there using her newfound time machine.

"Humor me," the captain smiled, walking around Riley slowly.

"I just kind of woke up there. Your guess is as good as mine."

"And these strange clothes," the captain said, pulling the back of Riley's t-shirt and snapping it back against her skin. "Is this how people in Boston dress nowadays?"

"I'm not exactly sure," Riley said, fishing for more information. "What year is it?"

"What *year?*" the captain said, cocking her head in surprise. "Just how long were sleeping in our storeroom, anyway?"

"Apparently it's been quite a long time since I left Boston," Riley said, understating the obvious.

"You don't look much worse for the wear for someone who's strayed so far from home," the captain said, leaning in to sniff the back of Riley's hair. "But to answer your question, the year is 1705, and you're aboard the Joan of Arc."

Riley paused for a moment, barely believing she'd been transported over three hundred years back in time aboard a maritime pirate ship.

"I couldn't help noticing that your crewmembers are all women," she said, peering at the guard.

"Yes," the captain nodded. "We're a group of slaves who managed to commandeer a pirate vessel while the regular sailors were distracted with other business. We find the open ocean and the freedom of the ship quite liberating after our previous experience."

"Slaves?" Riley said, trying to piece together the history from the captain's story.

"Prostitutes. Harlots. Women of ill repute. Pick your name for women forced to make a living servicing the needs of men."

Riley nodded, beginning to process the information.

"That's very impressive that you managed to free yourselves and create a new life on the sea," she said. "I like the name of your boat. Joan of Arc is one of my all-time heroes."

The captain hesitated for a moment, peering at Riley's tight ass in her jeans.

"This, coming from a frightened little girl found cowering in the storeroom of a pirate ship."

"I don't usually shy away from a challenge," Riley said, straightening her back. "Back home, I'm at the leading edge of a new kind of women's liberation."

The captain stopped behind Riley's back, noticing a bulge in her back pocket, lifting her smartphone out of her jeans.

"What's *this?*" she said, pinching her eyebrows at the strange object.

Riley paused for a long moment, wondering how she should respond. No one would believe that it was a telephone from the twenty-first century, let alone a magical time machine. The last thing she needed was someone stealing her one last hope for returning home.

"It's just a little toy I picked up in my travels."

"A *toy?*" the captain said, shaking it in her hand and sliding her fingers over the buttons along the side. "How does it work exactly?"

"I'm not quite sure," Riley said. "I'm still trying to figure it out myself..."

"Well, I think I'll keep it for now," the captain said, shoving it under the belt of her short skirt. Perhaps you'll be motivated to share a few more details about your mysterious life in Boston after spending some more time aboard our ship."

"What are you going to do with me?" Riley said, noticing the guard running her eyes up and down her body.

"You'll have to work to earn your keep on the ship like everyone else," the captain said. "Since you're the low woman on the pole, we'll start you off as a swabbie. Liza will take you to your crew quarters and get you set up. But if we find you hiding away or stealing any more of our precious cargo, you'll be dealt with in a far less forgiving manner."

Suddenly, there was a loud boom followed by someone on deck yelling *attack*, then a large plume of water sprayed up against the side of the ship, shaking it violently.

"Battle stations!" the captain nodded to the guard, reaching for her cutlass and pistol resting on her desk.

Then she peered at Riley with a lopsided grin, cocking her head to the side.

"Looks like we'll be putting you to work sooner than expected," she said. "You said you don't shy away from a battle. I hope you know how to handle a sword."

3

"A *what?*" Riley said, reaching out awkwardly to grasp the sword by its handle when the captain tossed it to her.

"All hands on deck," Kate said, motioning to Riley's guard, Liza. "You know the drill."

By the time everybody got topside, all hell had broken loose. While a fusillade of cannon fire erupted from the side of their ship, cannon balls from the attacking vessel sailed overhead, narrowly missing its mast and hull.

"Their cannons have longer range, captain!" the master gunner shouted, directing the cannon handlers to adjust their aim. "We're sitting ducks standing here broadside!"

The captain paused for a moment, watching the other ship's cannon balls slicing the water beside her.

"They would have hit us by now if they wanted to sink us," she said calmly. "We can't beat them trading fire. Prepare the crew for Operation White Flag."

"Operation White Flag?" Riley said, standing beside the captain, visibly shaking.

"They want to take our ship *undamaged*," Kate said. "They intend to board us."

"And you're going to *let* them?" Riley said, squinting at the much larger vessel bearing down on them. "Their ship is almost twice your size. How can you defend yourself against their greater numbers?"

"We have a few tricks up our sleeve," Kate smiled. "They won't be expecting a counterattack from a bunch of pussy sailors."

She turned to her master gunner and nodded.

"Wait until they're next to us before you fire the opening salvo. You know what to aim for. We're only going to have a few seconds to pull this off."

"Aye, aye, captain," the master gunner said, returning her attention to the gun crew.

While she passed along the captain's instructions, Riley peered at Kate, shaking her head.

"I thought you said you can't beat them trading cannon fire?"

"Not at this range," she replied. "But at close quarters, it's a different story."

"Won't they just reciprocate with superior firepower?"

"Not if we pretend to surrender first," the captain nodded, peering up to watch the white flag raised atop their mast. "As soon as they notice our ship is crewed with women, the only thing they'll be thinking about is shooting off their *other* cannons."

"Are you actually going to surrender?"

"Of course not. There's no such thing as honor among thieves. If we did, they'd just enslave us the same way we were before. On the open sea, it's every man – and woman – to themselves."

As the larger pirate vessel closed in on the women's ship,

the men on deck assembled alongside its gunwale, preparing to board their quarry. Riley noticed some of the women laying down heavy netting on deck while a few others pulled the main boom to the port side.

"There must be over a *hundred* of them," Riley she, staring at the sneering men. How can you hope to defeat them?"

"Be patient and keep your wits about you," Kate said. "First, we're going to even the odds a little, then we'll show them what it means to fight like a girl. Get ready to use that sword, because it's about to be busy on deck."

"But I don't know how to use a sword," Riley said, dangling the foil in her shaking hand.

"You seem like a capable lass," Kate said, peering at Riley's yoga-toned figure. "All you have to do is hold them off long enough for the rest of us to finish the job."

"Hold them off?" Riley said, shaking her head.

"Wait," Kate said, placing her hand over Riley's trembling wrist. "Just a few more moments..."

When the other ship closed within a few feet of the Joan of Arc and the men began jumping over the gap, Kate nodded to her first mate. Suddenly, the main boom swung rapidly across the deck, sending scores of sailors toppling overboard. The captain of the other vessel seemed surprised for a moment, then he ordered the next group over the rails. Kate waited until a group of twenty or so had amassed on deck, approaching the seemingly submissive women.

Then she motioned to her master gunner, and a barrage of cannon fire erupted, placing thick gashes in the other ship's lower hull, tilting it to one side, toppling their cannons into the water. When the boarding party realized the women had no intention of surrendering peacefully, they began rushing toward the crew with their swords drawn. Suddenly, the thick netting scooped them high up above deck, screaming in terror.

The captain of the other ship ordered the rest of his men to board the vessel, but as they streamed aboard, the women began to pick them off from their concealed hiding places. After their first pistol volley was exhausted, they emerged from their hiding places, engaging the invaders in one-on-one combat. Kate withdrew her cutlass from her belt and as she swiped it deftly from side to side, Riley crouched behind her, trying to duck the swinging blades and jostling bodies.

After a few moments, she noticed Liza defending herself against two men, and as they cornered her against one side of the deck, she glanced up at Riley with frightened eyes. Realizing that she'd be killed if someone didn't come to her rescue, Riley stepped toward the assailants, prodding one in the back with the tip of her sword. The man turned around and peered at the strangely dressed schoolgirl with an amused expression, then he lunged toward her with his sword.

Riley held her blade above her head with two hands trying to deflect his attack, but he soon pinned her toward the opposite side of the deck as she lowered herself onto to her knees. He lifted his sword to render the final blow then his eyes suddenly flew open as a spear lunged through his belly from behind. When he toppled onto the ground, Riley glanced up, noticing Liza standing behind him, holding her bloody sword.

"Come on," she said, holding out her hand to help Riley up. "The rest of the crew need our help. Stand at my back while we can watch out for one another."

As two angry pirates rushed toward them, Liza toppled the first one with a side-swipe to his thigh, then she sunk to her knees, slicing the other one's ankle. When he fell to the deck beside his comrade, she bound their hands behind their back, then she peered around the deck, noticing the fighting beginning to subside. Within minutes, the crew of the Joan of Arc had overpowered their opponents, pinning them toward the bow of the boat with their pistols drawn. When the last of the attackers dropped to his knees to signal surrender, Kate approached the leader, who peered back at her with a scowl.

"Are you the leader of this motley crew?" she said.

"I am," the man said, pressing his hand gingerly against a flesh wound on his side.

"What's your name?"

"Jack. Captain Jack."

"Well, Captain Jack, I'm Captain Kate. You and your crew are prisoners aboard the Joan of Arc. What's your business in these waters?"

"Same as you," he smiled. "Looking for easy marks. You know our credo. No prey, no pay."

"Except we don't prey on weaker opponents," Kate sneered. "That's something only you *men* like to do."

"Well now that you've defeated us," the captain huffed. "What are you planning to do with us?"

Kate turned to glance at his listing ship and nodded.

"Well you're sure as hell not going to stay here. We've had more than our fill of men on dry land."

"But our ship's no longer seaworthy," he said. "If you leave us out to sea, we're likely to sink and die."

"You should have thought of that before you attacked us first," Kate said.

"But you raised the *white flag*–"

"Come now, captain," Kate smiled. "You of all people know the other pirate code. There are no rules of warfare on the open sea."

Liza stepped toward the captive, pointing her sword at his neck.

"Why don't we just dump them overboard?" she said. "If they patch up their ship, they'll come after us again. With their larger draft and sails, it won't take long for them to overtake us."

Kate peered up at the fluttering sails hanging from the twin masts of the other pirate ship and nodded.

"Not if we disable their main mast. One against two will be no contest. But first, search the ship for any useful provisions. We'll leave them with just enough to make landfall."

4

After the women searched the other vessel and collected the salvageable material, Liza approached Kate, carrying a small map.

"What's *this?*" she said, turning it over in her hand, squinting at a hand-drawn diagram of South America. "It doesn't look like an official navigation map."

"I don't know," Liza said, placing her finger on a set of islands off the west coast. "But look at this notation. It might be worth investigating."

Kate's eyes focused on the spot marked with a red X and a sketch of a gold chest, then she lifted an eyebrow.

"Do you recognize this group of islands?" she said.

"No, but if there's gold there, it could be worth exploring."

"That's a long trip to make for an uncertain prize. Let's see if we can persuade our talkative captain to spill some more of his guts."

Kate approached Captain Jack, still bound up with the rest of his men, thrusting the picture in his face.

"Tell me about this map," she said. "How do you know there's gold there?"

Jack hesitated for a moment, wondering if he had more to gain or lose from disclosing more details.

"A Spanish galleon was sunk off the coast a few months ago," he said. "Most of their bounty was salvaged and brought to the mainland and buried in a secret location."

"Where did you find this map?"

"We found it aboard another vessel that picked up the sailors."

"Another one of your easy marks?"

"Something like that," Jack smiled.

"Why didn't they bring the gold *with* them aboard the other vessel?"

"I guess they wanted to keep it all for themselves."

"How much gold are we talking about exactly?" Kate asked.

"I'm not sure," Jack grinned. "But if it was really a Spanish galleon, it could be *millions*."

Kate took a moment to study the map, then she shook her head.

"Did these men tell you the precise location of these islands?"

"Yes," Jack nodded. "But if I tell you, you'll just leave me and my men drifting out at sea."

Kate peered at his side, noticing his hand covered in blood.

"If you don't tell me, you'll suffer a far faster fate."

"You already showed your hand when you didn't throw us overboard after you defeated us," Jack scoffed. "I think you're too soft to murder us in cold blood, like any other woman."

Liza suddenly approached the captain, bending the tip

of her sword into his wound, making him wince in pain.

"Leave him to me, captain, and I'll get it out of him," she said.

Kate paused for a moment to appraise her adversary, trying to assess his motivations. He was ruggedly handsome in a rakish sort of way, and the glimmer in his eye suggested he knew more than he was letting on.

"He's more useful to us *alive*," she said. "This map is pretty rough. He can help us navigate to the location and hopefully help us find the gold on the island."

Then she turned to face the captain.

"If we keep you on board and nurse you back to health, will you help us find these islands?"

"Yes, if you promise to share the spoils with me once we get there."

"Your share will be the same as all the rest of us. We share everything equally on this ship."

"What about the rest of my men?"

"They're of no use to us," Kate said. "We'll give them a dinghy and hopefully they can make it back to the mainland."

Jack paused to peer at his crew then he glanced at the crowd of scantily clad women surrounding him.

"Works for me," he smiled. "As long as you find a way to make my trip more comfortable."

After the captured sailors were returned to their vessel, Kate turned to her crew before releasing the tethers.

"Is there anything else you want to salvage from the ship before we set them adrift? This is your last chance to take what you want before we cast them off."

"Good riddance," Liza said, sneering at the sailors bound together at the base of the foremast.

"Alright," Kate said, preparing to throw them a pocket knife to untie themselves after they pushed off. "You boys better stay there for a little longer. There's going to be a few splinters flying around the foredeck pretty soon."

She motioned to her master gunner who angled one of their cannons halfway up the other boat's middle post.

"Wait!" Riley shouted, peering up at the large sails hanging from the tall mast. "Why don't we take their canvas?"

"Whatever would we do with those?" Kate said with a puzzled expression. "We don't have any room for them on our smaller masts."

"Like you said earlier," Riley nodded. "The larger the sail, the faster the ship. If they manage to repair the ship, they could follow us to retrieve the gold. It's a bit of extra insurance to ensure they don't get there first. Besides, I have an idea for how you could put that extra sailcloth to use on your ship."

"I thought you said you'd never been on a sailboat before?"

"I haven't," Riley grinned. "But I do have some experience *designing* sails."

Later that night after the women enjoyed a celebratory feast under the stars, Liza escorted Riley to the crew quarters to bed down for the night.

"I'm not sure what you're used to for sleeping arrangements up there in Boston," she said. "But here on our ship, we have to carve out every little space we can find."

She pointed to a row of swinging hammocks slung between stacked posts and motioned to an empty one near the bottom.

"You'll find the one on the bottom has the least motion from the rocking of the boat. We don't want you puking on the rest of us while you're still finding your sea legs."

"Thanks," Riley chuckled. "But speaking of bodily functions, where does a girl go to look after business around here? I didn't see a lavatory anywhere inside the ship."

A few of the other girls laughed while Liza smiled at Riley's naivety.

"The toilet is outside under the bowsprit at the head of the ship. We're not quite as modest as you landlubbers."

"So you, um, just go directly into the *sea*?"

"Like all the other sea creatures, yes," Liza said. "The ocean is really just one big toilet."

"Okay," Riley said, holding onto one of the bedposts for support. "Hopefully I won't fall overboard while I'm up there. See you in a bit."

"Don't hurry on our behalf. Better you unload your vapors up there in the open than down here in the hold. It's already stinky enough with twenty girls holed up in this tiny compartment."

After Riley finished her business and found her way back to the crew quarters, Liza and the rest of the girls were already lying peacefully in their hammocks, rocking gently with the motion of the boat in the calm seas. Liza had chosen the cot directly above hers, and as Riley gazed up at the outline of her naked figure lying in the swing, for the first time she began to realize how attractive she was. She'd been so preoccupied with her dragging her from the storeroom and fighting the other pirates that she hadn't stopped to appreciate her svelte figure and soft, feminine features.

"Glad you didn't fall through the cracks up there," Liza whispered from above. "With your tight little ass, I'm surprised you actually fit on the potty."

"It takes some getting used to, that's for sure," Riley chuckled. "Seeing the movement of the water directly below you is a bit intimidating."

"You get used to it pretty fast," Liza said. "It's actually more sanitary and fresh smelling than an indoor latrine."

"I guess there's quite a *few* things I'll have to get used to staying aboard the ship," Riley said, feeling her loins moistening as she peered up at Liza's swaying hips.

"I never thanked you properly for helping me earlier today when I was double-teamed by those pirates," Liza said. "That took a lot of courage stepping in when I was backed into a corner."

"It almost cost me my life," Riley chuckled. "If you hadn't saved the day, I would have been shark food for sure."

"I'll have to show you how to handle a sword tomorrow," Liza nodded. "You never know when we might get attacked again."

"So that little skirmish today wasn't just an outlier? How many pirate ships are there out here, anyway?"

"More than we care to count," Liza sighed. "With our smaller size, we're easy prey for larger and faster ships. We have to rely on our wits to outmaneuver and outlast the bigger crews."

"I might be able to help you with that," Riley smiled. "I've got an idea how we can put that extra sailcloth to good use."

"You mean for something other than making *hammocks*?" Liza chuckled.

"Yeah," Riley said, snaking her hand between her dripping thighs. "We might be able to fill them with some *other* heavenly bodies pretty soon..."

5

———

The following morning, the crew of the Joan of Arc enjoyed a hearty breakfast of quail eggs and dried meat. Riley noticed the captain of the other pirate ship was conspicuously missing, then she saw him chained on the front deck, close to the bow toilets. After the meal, Kate invited her back to her cabin to discuss her sail plan.

"So what's this great idea you have for using all that extra sailcloth?" she said, sitting behind her desk.

Riley peered at the large navigation maps laid out on her desk, wondering if the captain had stored her time machine there.

"I noticed that you use square sails on your masts," she said.

"Yes, like all the other ships of our day."

Riley paused, thinking it best to not yet reveal that she'd come from three hundred years in the future.

"If we use the extra material to sew larger sheets, we can hang the sails all the way from the top to the bottom of each mast."

"Won't that make them harder to handle?"

"Not if we make them in the shape of a *triangle*."

"Why would we want to do that?"

"A triangle-shaped sail harnesses the flow of the wind more effectively. You'll actually be able to sail *into* the wind, not just downwind."

"How is that even possible?" Kate said, pinching her eyebrows.

"Have you got some extra pen and paper I can use?"

"Sure," the captain said, pushing her maps over to the side and opening her logbook to an empty page.

Riley dipped her pen in the inkwell and began to sketch a three-dimensional image of a curved sail.

"With a triangular-shaped sail," she said, drawing arrows indicating the direction of the wind. "The air on the leeward side travels faster than the air on the windward side because of the curvature. This creates something called *lift*, which propels the vessel perpendicular to the direction of the wind."

"Where did you learn this?" Kate said, shaking her head as she peered at the drawing.

"The school I go to in Boston has a special department called aeronautics. It sounds complicated, but it works."

"Have you seen *other* sailboats using this design?" the captain said, still dubious of Riley's concept.

"Yes," Riley nodded. "The yacht club near my school holds races fairly regularly."

"But you haven't actually *been* on one?" Kate said.

"No, I just study the science."

Kate paused for a moment, staring at Riley's sketch and the direction of the arrows.

"Does this work sailing *downwind* as well?"

"No, that's mostly a function of your total sail area, as you mentioned earlier. Though I might be able to work on that too with some of the leftover sail material."

"So you're asking me to re-rig my entire ship based on a theory from someone who's never even set foot on a boat?"

"Let me try it on your foremast first," Riley nodded. "It will be quicker to build and will have minimal impact on your current sailing performance. If it doesn't work, you can just as easily put your old sails back up."

Kate paused for a moment, then she turned back to Riley and smiled.

"Do you know how to *sew*?" she said.

"Not really, but if you can supply enough needle and thread, I'm sure it can't be too difficult."

"I'll give you a couple of my best seamstresses to assist you," Kate said, peering at the maps on her table. "If you can help my boat sail into the wind, you could save us weeks navigating around the continent."

For the rest of the morning, Riley and two of the girls worked diligently, measuring, cutting, and sewing the new, larger sail for the ship's foreward mast. By midday, they'd fashioned a sleek new sheet, which they attached to the mast with the help of some of the other deck hands. With the sail neatly folded and resting on the boom, Riley peered toward Kate and the rest of the crew looking on with interest, and nodded.

"Are you ready to give this thing a try?" Kate said.

"Yes," Riley said. "But first you'll have to lower the sails on the main mast. Otherwise, they'll just push us backwards when we turn into the wind."

Kate swiveled her head around the horizon to search for

other pirate ships, then she motioned for her riggers to lower the main sails.

"We're going to be dead in the water with our sails down," she said. "I sure hope this idea of yours works. I don't want to be without power for very long."

Riley nodded then motioned for her assistants to begin raising the head of the sail slowly up the mast.

"If all goes well," she smiled. "This new sail will provide more power than all the *other* sails combined."

As it began to slowly fill with wind, the boom swung out to the side, causing the canvas to flap softly in the cross breeze. Riley motioned for some of the other sailors to grab hold of the rope attached to the end of the boom, then she glanced back at the captain.

"The boat will turn downwind when we begin to pull in the sail," she said. "Ask your rudder operator to steer it back into the wind as the sheet begins to fill. But not too far, otherwise the boom will swing to the other side."

Kate nodded toward her helmswoman, and as the boat slowly began to tack into the wind, the crew holding the fore-sail lines strained to hold it tight. After it had turned roughly forty-five degrees upwind, the ship suddenly began to pick up speed, slicing through the water with a heavy wake trailing behind the stern. While the girls holding onto the rope peered at Riley with wide eyes, the rest of the crew began to cheer loudly, hardly believing what they were seeing.

Kate walked up next to the tall sail, glancing up at it bending in the wind.

"I wouldn't have believed it if I hadn't seen it with my own eyes," she said, shaking her head. "Who would have thought a sailboat could sail into the wind? This changes everything."

As the helmswoman continued turning the ship further upwind, suddenly the sail began to flap and the boom began to swing across the deck.

"Coming about!" Riley shouted, pulling the captain down just in time to prevent her from being conked in the head.

As the ship lurched to one side and the rest of the crew scrambled to catch onto the nearest support, Kate looked at Riley with a bewildered expression.

"Sailing upwind presents a few new technical challenges," Riley nodded. "Not the least of which is learning how to trim the sails when you change course. But it shouldn't take too long for everybody to figure it out. The trick is to use the rudder to maintain the optimum angle, then only turn when you need to shift direction."

"Fascinating," Kate said, watching Riley and the others straining to hold onto the rope as the helmswoman steered their vessel back into the wind. "But I'm not sure I'll be able to spare enough sailors to maintain the lines if we outfit the *other* mast in the same way."

She glanced at Captain Jack, still chained up in the corner of the bowsprit a few feet away.

"We need enough crew to defend us if another pirate vessel gets any more bright ideas."

Riley motioned for the other women straining beside her to loosen their grip, and as the sail eased toward the lee side, she stood up, peering at her calloused hands.

"We'll need to connect the lines to something sturdy to bear the load," she nodded, rubbing her palms. "I might be able to fashion a makeshift winch to make it easier to adjust the tension, but for now we'll have to wrap the lines around these bollards to free up the crew."

"Not too shabby for someone who's never set foot on a sailboat," Kate said.

"Aeronautics is kind of my passion," Riley smiled. "I always dreamed about having my own boat someday. I guess this is about as close as I'm likely to get."

6

———

After Riley demonstrated how the new sail design could improve the speed of the boat, Kate mobilized some more women to sew the sail for the other mast while the rest of the crew practiced tacking and coming about. Riley used her engineering skills to design a pair of wooden winches on each side of the gunwales to hold and adjust the boom lines, and by mid-afternoon, the ship was steaming rapidly toward the eastern cape of South America.

"Who knew our mysterious stowaway had so many talents?" Liza smiled, strolling up beside Kate and Riley standing on the quarterdeck.

"She certainly seems wise beyond her years," Kate nodded. "It must be something in that New England water. Perhaps that's where I'll settle once we collect our bounty."

"You'd give up all this adventure on the sea?" Riley said.

"This ship was always just a means to an end," Kate said. "If there's as much gold on those islands as Captain Jack suggested, we'll all be able to retire and build respectable lives for ourselves back on the mainland."

Riley peered toward the front of the ship to glance at the pirate captain still chained to the bowsprit, watched over by an attractive crewmember carrying a sword.

"Do you think you can trust him?"

"We left his men with enough provisions to make land-fall," Kate nodded. "I can't imagine he'd cast his lot with us unless he knew there was something more valuable on the other side."

"Unless he was hoping to enjoy some of the *other* spoils aboard the ship during the journey there," Riley chuckled.

"Fat chance of that," Kate sneered. "We'll never succumb to men's prurient desires again. He can stay chained up next to the smelly toilets for the rest of the trip as far as I'm concerned."

Riley peered toward the handsome captain, noticing him smiling back at her.

"Why don't you at least let him join the rest of us for dinner?" she said. "Maybe we can extract a few more trade secrets using a carrot instead of a stick. There's more than twenty of you and only one of him. How much trouble can one man create surrounded by a troop of well-equipped sailors?"

"More than I care to imagine," Kate said. "The last thing we need right now is a bunch of pregnant crewmembers while we sail toward the most dangerous waters of the region."

"I thought we left most of the pirate threat behind us in the Caribbean?" Riley said, motioning toward the west.

"It's not *pirates* I'm worried about where we're headed," Kate said, watching her sails swing to starboard as the ship turned southward along the east coast of South America. "I've heard too many stories about the treacherous winds and currents of Cape Horn. I don't plan to join the legion of other ships in Davy Jones' Locker at the bottom of the sea."

"I guess we'll find out soon enough just how well these pretty sails perform in real sailing conditions," Liza smiled, drawing her sword. "In the meantime, how'd you like to polish some of your *other* sailing skills?"

"Using real swords?" Riley said, staring at Liza's glistening blade.

"We'll practice with bamboo sticks until you're able to defend yourself," she smiled, peering at Riley's tight jeans and t-shirt. "I wouldn't want to rip any of that fancy New England finery."

W hile Riley and Liza moved to the main deck to practice their fencing, Kate returned to her cabin to plot the ship's route southward toward Cape Horn. Later that evening, everyone convened in the mess hall for dinner, and Riley noticed Captain Jack escorted by two crewmembers, joining the rest of the group at the other end of the table.

"I thought we'd extend a little courtesy to our special guest this evening," Kate said, motioning to the other captain. "Even though I'm not sure he'd do the same for us if the battle had turned in the other direction."

"Much appreciated," Jack said, inhaling the scent of the freshly baked bread and chicken pot pie resting on the table. "It was getting a bit nippy up there on the forecastle. Not to mention as pleasant-smelling as down here close to the kitchen."

"Well don't get too used to it," Kate said, passing a jug of spiced rum around the table. "I still don't trust you as far as I can throw you. Which is a lot closer to *overboard* up there than down here."

"At least I'm having an opportunity to stay abreast of the latest sailing techniques while I'm tied up topside," he smiled. "That's quite an impressive rig you fashioned out of my old sails. I don't imagine you'll be overrun by another pirate ship with that new setup."

"We have our newest member of the crew to thank for that," Kate said, nodding toward Riley.

"Yes," Jack said, eyeing Riley's athletic figure in her tight t-shirt. "Although she seems awfully young to have so much sailing experience."

"Actually," Riley said. "This is my first time aboard a sailboat."

"Really?" Jack said, raising his eyebrows. "You seem to know your way around all that rigging pretty well for a land-lubber. Where are you from?"

"New England," Riley said.

"How did you manage to get all the way down here if you don't know how to *sail*?" Jack said, inspecting her clothes suspiciously.

"It's a bit of a long story," Riley chuckled.

"We've got a long trip ahead of us," Jack said, peering toward Kate at the other end of the table. "We can't tell pirate tales the *entire* way to our pot of gold."

Kate took a sip of her bumbo, gazing over the lip of her stein with steely eyes.

"If Riley's not comfortable sharing any more details of her private life," she said. "We will respect her wishes. If there's one thing we've learned gaining our liberation as free women, it's that men can no longer dictate their terms to us."

"I saw you practicing your fencing skills earlier," Jake

said, noticing the bruises on Riley's bare arms. "Are you sure you're ready for this life of a buccaneer?"

"It's definitely a little more *kinetic* than I had planned," Riley said, rubbing her welts. "But at least it's better than being sliced by a real sword."

"Yes," Jake said, rubbing his fingers over the stain on his shirt. "I can attest to that."

"How's your wound been healing?" Kate said.

"Quite well," he said, glancing at the ship's doctor. "Apparently your crew knows how to sew more than fancy sails. I should be back in fighting form in no time."

"Except your fighting days are over," Kate scowled. "At least until we find this mysterious treasure on the other side of the continent. I just hope you're not trying to pull another fast one, otherwise we might have to leave you to fend for yourself on those islands."

"I'm just as eager to find this gold as *you* are," he said. "And I'd like to settle down as much as the rest of you. Speaking of which, is possible to arrange more comfortable sleeping accommodations this evening? I hope you're not planning on keeping me chained up on deck for the rest of our trip?"

Kate paused for a moment while she peered around the table at the rest of her crew.

"This is a small ship, and I don't feel comfortable with you rubbing shoulders or anything *else* with my crew. You can stay in our locked storeroom if you prefer."

"How will I find my way to the *head*?"

"We'll give you a bucket to do your business. My crew already has enough distractions to escort you to the privy every few hours."

"I suppose it'll be an improvement on sleeping next to the bogger," he chuckled.

"Liza and Riley will escort you down to the room after dinner," Kate nodded. "You're welcome to join us at mealtimes as long as you keep your dick in your pants and behave yourself."

"I can't guarantee it won't pop out on its own accord once in a while," Jack smirked. "My mind's already been swimming with fantasies watching your shapely crew hauling in the ropes."

"As long as you keep it to yourself," Kate sneered. "I don't give a rat's ass what you do with your pecker."

7

———————

After they finished dinner, the night watch returned topside to steer the boat while the rest of the crew headed down to bed for the night. While Liza escorted Jack to the storeroom, Riley following close behind, staring at her sexy figure in her pirate uniform.

"Is this your main job aboard ship?" she smiled after Liza locked the door behind her. "Watching over prisoners in your ship's storeroom?"

"Actually," Liza said. "My official title is quartermaster, second in command to the captain. She put me in charge of watching over the prisoners because of my special fighting skills."

"Yes," Riley said, rubbing her sore bruises. "You aren't fond of giving much quarter to your captives, are you?"

"I'm sorry," Liza said, pausing in the passageway. "Did I hurt you earlier today?"

"Actually," Riley said, tapping her arm gingerly. "I don't think you missed a single place on my body with your so-called *practice* blows."

"Oh?" Liza said, cornering Riley against the wall while pinching her skin softly. "Does it hurt here?"

"Yes," Riley nodded.

"How about *here*?" Liza said, sliding her hand slowly up Riley's arm and squeezing her shoulder.

"Definitely yes," Riley winced.

"What about here?" Liza said, cupping Riley's left breast.

"Not quite as much–" Riley smiled, feeling her nipples growing erect.

"How about *here*?" Liza said, placing her hand between Riley's thighs and squeezing her crotch.

"That's one spot you managed to miss," Riley grunted.

"That can be taken care of easily enough," Liza smiled, opening the door to the ship's weapons locker and pulling Riley down atop a pile of burlap bags.

When Riley felt Liza's breasts pressing against her, she tore at her clothing, pulling off her leather vest and ruffled blouse and kissing her hard on the lips. It had been a long while since she'd felt the warm skin of another lover caressing her, and after all the sexual tension of the previous night and Liza's pounding her with her practice baton, she hadn't realized how aroused she'd become.

"I've been dying to get you naked from the moment I laid eyes on you," Liza panted, thrusting her thigh between Riley's legs.

"You have a funny way of showing it," Riley said, squeezing Liza's ass in her hands.

"That was the only way I could actually touch you with the captain watching," Liza smiled.

"You could have just *asked* me," Riley said, pulling Liza's mouth down toward hers. "I was wet all night watching your sexy body rocking above me in the crew quarters."

"I thought I heard more than the usual groaning and

snoring down there. I'm surprised you didn't wake up all the other girls up with your heavy breathing."

"Well, we don't have to worry about any of that here," Riley said, rolling on top of Liza and spreading her knees over her hips, grinding her pussy against her mound.

"Mmm," Liza groaned, raising her knees up around Riley's waist. "Rub that dripping quim against me. You have no idea how much I need this."

"You don't take advantage of the *other* girls in our little crew compartment once in a while?" Riley grinned.

"Sometimes," Liza said, pressing her vulva against Riley's burning pussy. "But those hammocks aren't exactly conducive to bed play with two or more people."

"Now that you've got a horny cock waiting for you in the adjacent storeroom, you shouldn't have trouble satisfying your sexual needs for the next few weeks."

"I prefer the soft skin of a *woman*," she grunted, rolling her hard clit over Riley's.

"Me too," Riley moaned, listening to the sound of their pussies slapping together while the ship rocked gently underneath them.

"Have you got any *other* surprises you've been holding out on us?" Liza moaned, squeezing Riley's waist between her quivering legs.

"You mean about sailing?"

"Or anything else about sneaking aboard a female pirate ship."

"Other than feeling the rush of the wind in my sails and the swing of the boom between my legs..."

"Are you getting ready to come about soon?" Liza smiled.

"Yes," Riley panted, rocking her slippery ass over Liza's upturned thighs. "You better hold onto the lines pretty tight. Cause I'm about to produce a different kind of backwash–"

Suddenly, Riley grunted loudly as she mashed her pussy hard against Liza, squirting hard jets over her open hole, drenching her ass and pussy with her erotic juices. When Liza felt Riley gushing over her splayed legs, she crossed her feet over her back, pulling their bodies tighter together as they grunted and shook atop one another. When they finally came down from their powerful climaxes, Riley collapsed on top of Liza's heaving body, feeling her heart beating against her chest.

"Wow," Liza panted. "You really *are* from another place. Where did you learn to do *that*?"

"Let's just say aeronautics isn't the *only* thing I've been studying in Boston," Riley smiled. "College life has opened my eyes to a whole new world of possibilities."

8

For the next two weeks, the ship steamed directly southward toward the tip of South America while the crew practiced tacking and jibing using the new sail configuration. Riley and Liza took as many chances as they dared stealing away for private trysts, spending the rest of their time working on Riley's fencing skills. By the time they reached the chilly waters of the Antarctic Ocean, she'd already graduated to using real foils, holding her own against the more experienced quartermaster.

As they neared the corner of the continent, Kate noticed a strong eastward current, and the crew had to use all of their sailing skills to keep the ship pointed into the wind, tacking every couple of minutes to maintain a westward course. By the time they passed around the southern tip, the strong westerly winds funneled by the meeting of the two continents had whipped up waves close to fifty feet, and the Joan of Arc whipsawed from crest to trough, struggling to maintain its course.

While Kate, Liza, and Riley struggled to maintain their

balance on the raised quarterdeck, the ship's boatswain staggered toward them to report on the ship's condition.

"Captain," she shouted over the howling wind. "I think we should trim the sails lest they tear in these strong winds. If we lose the ability to steer the boat, we'll turn broadside against the waves."

"I understand the risk," Kate said, peering up at the straining sails against the blinding sleet and hail. "But with these strong currents, we need as much forward power as we can get to make any headway."

Kate turned to Riley holding onto a stanchion with white hands, squinting her eyes.

"How strong are the seams in those new sails?" she said. "Can they withhold this kind of pressure?"

"I'm not sure," Riley said. "I hadn't expected winds like these when we patched them together. I'd be more concerned about the connections to the mast. The rings and loops are the real weak point. If you can lower them partway, that will take some pressure off the joints."

Kate turned to the boatswain and nodded.

"Reef the main sail halfway," she instructed. "We'll use the front sail to do the heavy lifting. But keep an eye on the connections to make sure they're holding fast. If you see them weakening, ease further at your discretion."

"Aye, aye, captain," the boatswain said, holding onto the gunwales as she lurched her way forward over the pitching deck.

Kate peered up at the large black cloud rolling in from the west, then turned to Riley with a worried expression

"I think you should go below deck until this blows over," she said. "You don't have as much experience as the rest of the crew, and you could be washed overboard in these pitching seas."

"You need all the hands you can spare on deck," Riley shouted back. "I didn't sign up for this just to shy away at the first sign of bad weather."

"Well at least lash yourself onto something secure then," Kate said, flexing her legs to maintain her balance as the ship pitched and rolled from side to side.

Riley grabbed a long mooring line behind the helm, and just as she finished tying a double knot securely around her waist, she looked up, hearing a loud tear coming from the area of the forecastle. She only had enough time to see the front sail slicing in half before a giant wave washed up on deck, sweeping her over the gunwales.

While she tumbled headlong over the side of the ship, all she could hear was the agonized scream of Liza rushing toward her before she fell into the icy water below. At first, she was too shocked to feel anything, but as her bruised body began to slap against the side of the ship with the taut rope digging into her waist, she suddenly felt the grip of the churning water closing in around her.

"Woman overboard!" Kate yelled on deck, and as five sailors scrambled to her aid on the rear deck, trying to pull her aboard, Riley peered into the inky darkness, noticing a huge white object approaching the listing ship.

"Iceberg!" she shouted, pointing her numb finger in the direction of the towering behemoth.

As the giant block began scraping against the side of the hull, Liza looked down at her with frightened eyes, screaming to her crewmates.

"Pull!" she shouted. "Pull with everything you've got! If that iceberg hits Riley, it'll break the line and we'll lose her forever!"

As Riley began to feel herself pulled out of the water, she watched the floe coming toward her like a freight train, and just before it passed, she hit her head hard against the wall of ice before bouncing back on board.

The last thing she remembered before passing out was the puddle of blood pooling around her body while Liza kneeled over her, cradling her head.

9

———

When Riley woke up, she found herself lying in a soft bed in the captain's cabin while the ship rocked heavily from side to side.

"What happened?" she said, noticing Kate sitting on the edge of the bed, holding a cup of hot tea.

"You hit your head when you fell overboard," Kate said. "You're lucky to be alive. That was an awfully close call."

"The sail, the iceberg..." Riley groaned, touching her aching head. "What about the *ship*? Did it suffer much damage?"

"Don't worry about the ship right now," Kate chuckled, handing her the tea. "Right now, you need to warm up. You're still suffering from hypothermia."

"How did you manage to gain control the ship with the torn sail? Was the hull badly damaged?"

"Thank heavens the main sail held," Kate nodded. "With a bit of skilled seamanship, we managed to keep the ship righted. The iceberg just made a glancing blow. It was a close call for *everyone*."

"So it's *true* what they say about Cape Horn," Riley said.

"I should have warned you about the Bounty. We should have taken the Magellan Straight."

"The *what?*" Kate said, looking at Riley like she was dreaming. "Are you referring to the pot of gold we're heading toward?"

"Oh, never mind," Riley said, suddenly remembering the events she was describing were still decades into the future.

"Rest up," Kate said, pulling the covers higher over Riley's naked body.

"What happened to my clothes?" she said.

"We couldn't very well leave them on with you shivering the way you were after we pulled you out of the water," Kate smiled.

"What about Liza and the rest of the crew? Is everybody safe?"

"Yes," Kate said, stroking the tangled hair around Riley's patched head wound. "They're needed on deck until we get through this storm. We should be through the worst of it by daybreak. I'll check in on you a little later. Now try to get some sleep."

R iley dozed off for a few hours and when she awoke, she noticed Kate undressing beside her, preparing to turn in for the night.

"What time is it?" Riley said, bundling up under the covers.

Kate turned to her looking surprised, then she glanced at her pocket watch.

"Four a.m., give or take. Although that's the *last* thing you should be worried about right now. How are you feeling?"

"Still cold and sore," Riley said, feeling her body shivering under the blankets.

"It's going to take a while for your core temperature to return to normal," Kate nodded. "Maybe I can help with that."

She pulled off the rest of her clothes and before she nestled in next to Riley, Riley had just enough time to scan her voluptuous figure and dark bush between her legs.

"Mmm," Riley purred, wrapping her legs around Kate's hips to maximize their body contact. "You're a lot warmer and softer than these scratchy sheets."

"I don't suppose it's quite as comfortable as you're used to up there in the big city," she said, holding Riley tightly as she pressed their tits together.

"Oh, this is *plenty* comfortable enough," Riley sighed, feeling her pussy beginning to throb from the sensation of Kate's soft muff caressing her mound. "I can feel my core warming up already."

Kate leaned in to kiss Riley, and as the two women began grinding their hips together, Kate nibbled her way down Riley's stomach, pausing at her trimmed pubis to scrape her cheeks over her stubble. Riley parted her legs, inviting her to go lower, and when Kate's lips encircled her burning clit, she moaned, pulling her head harder toward her crotch.

"You're certainly not cold down *here*," Kate purred, sucking her button into her mouth.

"Neither are you," Riley panted, tilting her dripping pussy up toward Kate's face. "If this is my reward for falling overboard, I'll have to go topside during heavy storms more often."

"This top side is plenty good enough for me," Kate chuckled, rolling her tongue over Riley's twitching pearl while Riley rocked her hips against the captain's face.

"You're going to push me over a *different* edge pretty soon if you keep doing that," Riley grunted, feeling her pleasure beginning to spread in her pelvis.

"Never fear," Kate said, placing her hands around Riley's flexing buttocks. "I'll be here to catch you this time."

"I should warn you," Riley moaned, feeling herself nearing the tipping point. "Things can get pretty wet down there when I climax..."

"I'm used to wet conditions," Kate nodded, encouraging Riley to let go. "I'm the captain of all-women pirate ship, after all."

"Nghhh," Riley groaned, feeling her climax suddenly wash over her.

Kate's head jerked when she felt Riley's juices gushing over her face, but she held onto her until she finished shaking, then she slowly inched her way back up beside the pretty co-ed.

"That was almost as intense as the storm we just passed through," she grinned, kissing Riley softly on her lips. "You're full of surprises, aren't you?"

"Sorry about that," Riley said. "I've never been very good at controlling myself when I come. Especially when someone's licking me so expertly."

"Except this isn't the *first* time you've felt a woman's lips on your pussy, is it?"

"What makes you think–?"

"Come now, my little stowaway," Kate smiled, circling a finger around Riley's erect nipple. "This is a small ship after all. It's pretty hard to keep a secret with twenty women sleeping on top of one another."

"You don't mind?" Riley said.

"Of course not," Kate grinned. "It's healthy for my sailors to release their sexual tensions. And with no men on board, it's only natural to find comfort wherever we can find it."

"Well technically, there *is* one man on board..."

"True," Kate said. "And I may avail myself of his services if I get desperate enough."

"I thought you said you'd had your fill of men back on land?"

"That's when we didn't have any control over who we had sex with. Out here on our own ship, we're masters of our dominion."

"Well I could get used to all this pitching and rolling," Riley said, snaking her hand under the covers to caress Kate's furry bush.

Kate returned the gesture, pausing over Riley's clipped mound as she pulled her head back in curiosity.

"What's the story behind your trimmed quim?" she said, scratching the stubble with her fingertips. "Is this another strange custom of you society girls up there in New England?"

"I think it's more a sign of the *times*," Riley smiled, sliding her finger into Kate's slit. "Maybe it's just another way of signaling our liberation from men. You know, because men are more hairy, it's a way of highlighting our more delicate features."

"Well I like it," Kate said, squeezing Riley's clit between her fingers. "Less of a mouthful of hair when I go down on your pretty cunny."

"Speaking of," Riley said, shifting lower under the covers. "Isn't it *your* turn for a little fun?"

"In due course," Kate said, pulling Riley closer toward her. "Tell me about this Magellan character you mentioned earlier, and this ship you call the Bounty. Where did you hear about these explorers?"

"The usual history books," Riley said, wrinkling her forehead.

"It seems that we're reading different history books," Kate said, twisting Riley's nipples firmly with her fingers. "Because I've never heard of either of these boats. And how could you possibly know about a different passage through these parts?"

"Well, I go to a pretty big school up there in Boston," Riley smiled. "They have a big library."

"Um, hmm," Kate nodded with a sly smile. "Now tell me how you *really* got aboard my ship..."

10

———

W hile Riley recuperated from her injuries, the Joan of Arc steamed north along the west coast of South America, following the strong trade winds pushing up from Patagonia. After a few days, she joined Kate on the top deck, marveling at the majestic sight of the snow-capped Andes mountains rising twenty thousand feet above the cobalt-blue sea.

"Now *that's* a sight for sore eyes," she said, watching the newly repaired sails luffing softly in the southerly breeze.

"Not too shabby," Kate nodded, standing on the quarter-deck, admiring the view. "It seems that not *every* part of this continent is as dark and foul-tempered as Cape Horn."

"I see you managed to patch up the sails," Riley smiled.

"Yes," the captain said, watching the booms angling far over the starboard side. "Although your new design doesn't deliver quite the same advantages sailing downwind."

"How much longer until we reach your mysterious treasure island?"

"Another week maybe, if these winds continue at their current strength."

"Well at least we've got a nice view to keep us distracted until then."

"Are you talking about the mountains, or some of the *other* topographical features?" Kate grinned, noticing Liza approaching Riley with a bright smile.

Suddenly, the lookout in the crowsnest atop the main mast shouted below, pointing south.

"Ship ahoy!"

Kate pulled out her spyglass, swinging around to focus the lens.

"It's a big one," she said, telescoping the shaft. "Three masts. Looks like a man o' war."

"Is it flying a banner?" Liza said, taking up position beside the captain.

"The skull and crossbones," Kate nodded.

"Where did they come from?" Liza said, shaking her head. "I thought we shook everyone on the other side of the peninsula."

"They must have followed us around the cape."

"What's our plan?" Liza said, squinting into the distance at the pursuit vessel. "We'll be no match for their much larger complement of guns and crew."

"Our only chance is to outrun them."

"How can we do that with the sail at our backs?" Liza said, pinching her eyes. "These sails aren't much use to us downwind."

Kate turned to Riley with a worried expression.

"You said you had another trick up your sleeve to help us sail downwind. Is there anything you can do before they overtake us?"

"How much time have we got?" Riley said.

"Two hours at best."

"I might be able to pull it off if you give me enough crew.

We still have all your old sail material in the hold. That should give us more than enough coverage to outpace them."

"But where will you *put* it?" Kate said. "All of our mast space is already filled."

"Let me figure that out," Riley said. "Right now, I just need more seamstresses."

"Take as many as you like," Kate nodded. "With the wind blowing directly from the south, we don't need as many riggers managing the sails."

Kate turned toward Liza, gripping her shoulder firmly.

"Can you mobilize the crew and oversee the construction? We're not going to have much time."

"No worries, captain," Liza smiled. "I'm used to get things done quickly with our new engineer."

After the women retrieved the old sails from the storeroom, the entire crew positioned themselves in a circle on the main deck, laying out the cloth and sewing it into a large, symmetric triangle. Within an hour or so, the larger pirate ship had closed to within fifteen hundred yards of the Joan of Arc, and suddenly a loud burst of cannon fire erupted as the water around its stern began to rock the boat.

"How's it going down there?" Kate yelled to Riley and Liza, trying to steer the ship out of the line of fire.

"We're almost ready," Riley nodded. "Just a couple more minutes."

"We might not have that many," Kate said, peering through her spyglass at the approaching ship.

"Okay," Riley said, directing the girls to fasten three lines to the corners of the sail, making sure the cringles were properly reinforced. "We're good to go!"

Kate gazed down from the helm, peering at the giant sheet covering her entire deck.

"Where in heaven's name are you going to hang that thing?"

"To the foremast," Riley said. "There's still plenty of available space in front of the bow."

The women folded the sail and carried it up to the forecastle, where they tied two ends to opposite sides of the bow. Then Riley peered at Liza, handing her the third end.

"Who's your ablest crewmember to tie this to the top of the mast?"

Liza glanced at the roiling waves rocking the ship, watching the cannon balls slicing closer to the hull.

"We haven't got much time to arm wrestle over it," she said, hopping onto the shroud at the base of the mast and climbing hand over hand up the ratlines toward the top.

When she reached the crest, she wrapped the cord around the tip, tying it securely with a strong knot. The women on the lower end released their lines to ease the pressure on the sail, then Riley instructed them to rake in the sheets and tie them off. Suddenly, the big spinnaker filled with air, puffing forward over the bow like a bloated belly, and the ship began to pick up speed, slowly moving away from the pursuing pirate ship.

When they were no longer within cannon range, Kate joined Riley and the other sailors on the forward deck, admiring their handiwork.

"Now *there's* another sail configuration I've never seen before," she smiled. "I'm going to have to make some time to read those books in your school library."

Liza stepped down from the base of the mast, squinting over the stern with a worried expression.

"But we haven't got anywhere to hide out here on the open sea," she said. "What if that ship is going to the same place we're headed?"

Kate nodded, glancing at the rest of her anxious crew.

"I think it's time we had another chat with our charming captain to see if he's hiding any other secrets from us."

After Kate and Riley returned to the captain's cabin, Liza escorted Captain Jack toward the rear quarters, where they all crowded around the navigation maps spread out on her desk.

"Who *else* knows about this treasure?" Kate said, peering at Jack.

"Quite a few, I expect," he smirked. "It sounds like some of them have *already* taken up the chase from the cannon fire I heard earlier."

"Who'd have the resources to commission a man o' war?"

Jack turned toward Kate with a surprised expression.

"If my men returned to the mainland and spread the word about the gold on this island, it wouldn't take long to attract the attention of the big-timers. The only pirate I know of with a ship that size is Blackbeard."

"*Blackbeard*," Kate sighed. "Great. Just who we need on our tail right about now."

She glanced at the hand-drawn treasure map, then pulled a larger map closer toward her.

"Do you know anything about this archipelago? How tall is the landmass? Will it offer any protection for us to hide behind while we search for the treasure?"

Jack paused as his eyes darted over the map.

"I've never even *been* on this side of the continent," he said, shaking his head. "But the captured sailors said the gold was buried at the side of a tall bluff. So there must be some elevation to speak of."

Kate peered outside her rear window, watching the larger ship fade off into the distance.

"I just hope we'll be able to find it before Blackbeard catches up with us and unleashes the full fury of his guns," she said.

11

When the Joan of Arc reached the archipelago shown on the treasure map, they circled around the largest island for cover, then headed for the northern-most cay marked with the X. As the crew gathered along the side of the ship, they marveled at the abundant wildlife lounging on the beaches, seemingly oblivious to the sight of the big ship passing nearby. Huge colonies of black iguanas bathed lazily in the sun while blue-footed boobies performed elaborate mating dances and puffy-red frigate birds circled overhead.

Not far offshore, the turquoise-blue water teemed with a plentiful array of colorful sea creatures, from lumbering sea turtles to playful dolphins and darting penguins, flying through the shallow water like drunken acrobats. As Riley observed the incredible nature display, it occurred to her that she was witnessing the isolated paradise of the Galapagos Islands over a hundred years before Charles Darwin discovered it.

"It's beautiful, isn't it?" Liza said, leaning over the gunwale beside Riley.

"I've never seen anything like it," Riley nodded, looking further inland. "And from the barren appearance of the landscape, it looks like hardly anyone *else* has either."

"Maybe this is where I'll settle down after we collect the gold," Liza said. "No men, abundant food, and crystalline, warm water. This is my idea of Shangri-La."

"I'm not sure all these tranquil creatures would welcome the intrusion," Riley chuckled. "Now I see why Darwin chose this place as the laboratory for his research. With no human disruption, the animals are free to breed and move about with impunity. No wonder there's such a diversity of wildlife here."

"Darwin *who*?" Liza said, shaking her head. "You've heard of these islands?"

"Only from my biology textbooks. These islands are the cradle of evolution."

"Evolution?"

"It's kind of hard to explain," Riley chuckled, thinking it best not to create any more suspicion about her origin.

"You sure know a lot for a someone from the other side of the world."

Kate saddled up next to Riley and Liza on the railing, surveying the passing land formations.

"So, this bluff you were talking about earlier," she said as Captain Jack joined them. "Did the sailors give you any more hints as to what it looked like?"

"They said it was a dark spiky rock at the side of a crescent-shaped beach."

"Well, there's a lot of beaches on this island," Kate said, shaking her head. "And the only dark spiky things I see are those strange-looking reptiles lounging in the sand."

"Over there!" Riley said, pointing to a tall promontory

jutting out to sea on the small adjacent islet. "That's a pretty unforgettable landmark."

Kate instructed her crew to set anchor a few meters offshore, then a small landing party lowered a skiff, rowing toward the beach. When they stepped ashore, the big black iguanas hardly seemed perturbed as giant hard-shelled tortoises ambled slowly nearby.

"The red X is positioned over the bluff," Kate said, holding the treasure map. "Any more clues as to the precise location of the gold?"

"The sailors said it was in an underwater cave," Jack said, peering along the coastline for any sign of a hollow.

"I don't see anything other than the sandy beach and a cliff descending to the water," Liza said, shaking her head.

Riley peered toward the bluff, noticing the waves making a hissing noise as they crashed against the cliff.

"There seems to be some kind of air pocket over there," she said, pointing toward the bubbling water. "Why don't we swim over and see what we can find?"

As they waded into the water, a band of playful seal pups darted between their legs, curious about the identity of strange interlopers. When they lowered themselves under the surface, penguins flew past them like underwater bats while a school of golden rays drifted slowly by. For Riley, it seemed like a giant seaquarium – one where she was free to wade in and mingle with the curious sea creatures.

While she played with the cute seal pups circling around her body, Kate tapped her on her shoulder, motioning for them to continue moving ahead. When they reached the base of the bluff, they noticed an underwater vent, and when they swam through it, they emerged into a small cavern illuminated with thin shafts of light slicing through from the overhead cracks. The cavern had a small beach, and as they pulled themselves up on the sand, they peered around the chamber, looking for any sign of the treasure chest.

"Are you sure this wasn't some kind of elaborate ruse intended to send us on a wild goose chase?" Kate said, frowning at Captain Jack.

"They seemed just as eager as the *rest* of us to retrieve the gold," Jack nodded.

"I don't see any treasure chest, do you?"

"Maybe they *buried* it to make it harder to find."

Riley peered around the cave, noticing an oddly shaped piece of driftwood sticking out of the sand.

"If they buried it, wouldn't they have to place some kind a marker?" she said.

She got down on her hands and knees and began scooping the sand around the base of the stick. After a few minutes, she felt something hard and she swiped the grains to the side, revealing the top of an ornate metal box glistening in the overhead sunlight.

"I found something!" she said as the rest of the group joined her, pawing at the sand to uncover a huge, bejeweled chest.

When they opened the lid, the entire cavern sparkled from the illumination of thousands of gold coins piled to the rim of the chest. Kate dipped her hands into the pile, flipping some of the coins over in her fingers.

"Their doubloons and escudos," she nodded. "Minted in Spain from pure gold. Your captured sailors weren't kidding."

"There must be millions in here," Liza said, scooping up the coins and letting them drop like a waterfall from her fingers.

"Maybe even *billions* in today's dollars," Riley said.

"I'm pretty sure this stuff has enormous value just about *everywhere*," Jack chuckled, inspecting the coins more carefully.

"Yes," Kate said, leaning back on her hands as she peered toward the entrance to the cave. "But now we have a new dilemma. How are we going to get all this gold out of here? This chest must weigh five hundred pounds, and if we try to take it out piecemeal, it'll take us hours or days to bring it all back to the ship. If Blackbeard knows about this treasure too, he could catch up with us any moment."

"What about the dinghy?" Liza said.

"How would we get it in here?" Kate said. "If we submerged it, we'd never get it back out."

"Not unless we turned it *upside down*," Riley grinned.

"What?" Kate said, looking at Riley like she had two heads. "Why would we do that?"

"It would create an air pocket underneath," Riley said. "If we lashed the chest on top, it might create just enough buoyancy to float it out through the hole."

Kate paused as she peered at Riley, shaking her head.

"It might just work," she said. "But we'll have to hurry. I don't know how much time we'll have before Blackbeard finds us hiding out on this side of the island."

12

The group returned to the beach to retrieve the dinghy then they filled it with water, passing it through the underwater gap to lift it into the cave. Then they turned it over and lashed the chest of gold over the keel, tipping the boat to fill it with just enough water to partially submerge it. As they pressed their bodies on top of the overturned hull, it lowered through the hole, where they steered it back onto the beach. When they reached the shore, they quickly righted the skiff and rowed it back toward their ship, where the crew lowered some ropes and hauled the treasure aboard.

When Kate raised the lid, the women stared at the pile of shimmering coins with wide eyes, then they shouted with joy, interlocking their arms and dancing a jig on the main deck. Suddenly, a loud boom sounded from the stern, and a cannon ball sliced through the rear quarterdeck, sending splinters flying everywhere.

"Raise the sails!" Kate shouted, watching the giant man o' war rounding the bend, heading straight toward them.

"Point into the wind! We need to put some distance between us before they sink us!"

While the women hastily raised the sails, Kate grabbed the wheel of the ship, trying to maintain a narrow profile against the larger ship's firing guns. As cannon balls whizzed past, the sails began to fill with wind and the ship angled southward, slicing through the churning waves. After fifteen minutes, the other ship receded into the distance, and Liza, Riley, and Jack joined the captain at the helm.

"That was a close one," Liza said, shaking her head. "Did we suffer much damage to the ship?"

"It looks like I'll have a bit more ventilation in my captain's quarters for a while," Kate said, peering over the side of the hull at the gash in the rear quarterdeck. "But at least we're still seaworthy."

"So where do we go now?" Jack said, noticing the other ship still trailing behind. "I don't think Blackbeard's going to give up that easily."

"As long as Riley's sails can hold in this strong breeze, we should be able to lose them around the horn. With our speed advantage, they won't be able to catch up."

"What's the plan when we get back around the other side?" Riley said. "Once the word gets out that we've captured the treasure, every pirate vessel in the Caribbean will be gunning for us."

Kate paused for a moment, studying Riley's pretty face.

"Why don't we head up *your* way?" she smiled. "Nobody will be expecting us that far north and it shouldn't take long for us to assimilate into your tea and crumpets crowd with all this extra money."

"Works for me," Riley nodded. "Though I'd hardly say I'm part of the tea and crumpets crowd."

That night, the foursome regrouped in the captain's cabin for a celebratory dinner while the rest of the crew kept a lookout for other ships.

"I'd like to make a toast," Kate said, raising a goblet of wine over the dinner table. "To Captain Jack, without whom we would never have found our pot of gold at the end of the rainbow."

"It's kind of ironic," Liza nodded, grudgingly raising her glass. "That the same men who once kept us as concubines have finally helped us find our way back to genteel society."

"Well, in my defense," Jack smiled, taking a swig of his wine. "It wasn't me *personally* who exploited you, though I for one will be happy to see you resuming peaceful lives."

"What about *you*, our mysterious stowaway?" Kate said, turning to Riley. "What will you do with your share of the fortune when you return to Boston?"

Riley paused for a moment, realizing that the city she'd be returning to would look nothing like the modern metropolis she'd left a few weeks before.

"I'm not sure I'll be able to carry it all back with me to be honest," she said. "I don't know what I'd do with all that money, anyway. I'm just a curious engineering student who likes to invent things and dream about exciting adventures."

"Well speaking of *inventions*," Kate said, excusing herself to retrieve something from her desk. "I still haven't any idea what this fancy machine is that you brought with you onto our ship, but I'd say you've more than earned the right to have it returned after everything you've done to help us."

When Kate handed Riley her smartphone, she turned it over in her hands, wondering if it even still held a charge. As much as she'd loved her adventure on the high seas, she was eager to get back to her normal life and relax after the excitement of the last few weeks.

"Thanks," she said, putting the device in her back pocket. "But I really didn't do that much. You women are the *real* heroes, pulling yourselves out of bondage and setting the standard for female empowerment."

13

———

While the foursome drank late into the night sharing tales of adventure on the sea, Riley noticed Jack and Kate growing fonder of one another, finding fellowship in their mutual roles as pirate captains. After the fourth bottle, Riley and Liza decided to turn in for the night, weary from all the excitement of the day. As they made their way back to the crew cabin, Liza paused in the passageway, placing her arm on the side of the bulkhead.

"Are you sure you want to go back and sleep with the rest of the crew tonight?" she smiled.

"Actually," Riley said, stepping closer toward her. "I was hoping to have one more night alone with you."

"Only *one*?" Liza said.

"I'm not sure how many more days we'll have together."

"Well, it's going to take a few weeks to sail around this continent," Liza smiled, unlatching the door to their private hideaway. "That should give us plenty of time to enjoy the fruits of our spoils."

As they tumbled onto the thick spinnaker sail folded in

the corner, Riley tugged at Liza's pirate uniform, kissing her passionately.

"This big sail of yours is good for more than just sailing *downwind*," Liza panted. "I haven't slept on a bed this soft in ages."

"Were you only planning on *sleeping* on it?" Riley grinned.

"Fuck no," Liza grunted, rolling overtop of Riley's naked body and kneeling between her thighs, pressing her dripping pussy against Riley's warm snatch. "I was kind of hoping to feel something *else* blowing over me before the night is over."

After the two women made love for the next hour, Liza rolled over and fell fast asleep beside Riley, who was still wide awake peering at her mysterious smartphone. She still had no idea exactly how it worked, or even if it would start up again, but when she pressed the On button on the side, the screen suddenly lit up, displaying the familiar image of the swirling funnel. As it began to shake more violently in her hand, the funnel began rising once again above the glass surface. Riley could feel the power of the vortex pulling her toward it, and she reached out to touch Liza's cheek before raising her other hand up to the edge of the funnel.

Suddenly, she felt herself pulled back into the cloud, tumbling through the three-dimensional portal, unsure where or when she would land. After a few minutes, she dropped onto a rickety bed in a small wood-framed room, overlooking the main street of a dusty frontier town.

Not long after, a man wearing a cowboy hat and a pair of

Colt revolvers on his belt entered the room, closing the door behind him. When he saw Riley's naked body lying on top of the sheets, he smiled and unbuckled his belt, advancing toward the shaking schoolgirl.

"I haven't seen *you* around here before," he smirked, stepping out of his cowboy boots and unstrapping his chaps. "But you'll do just fine satisfying my appetite–"

"What? No..." Riley said, standing up to defend herself against the man's advance. "I don't know who you think I am, but I'm not going to have sex with you."

"No?" the man sneered. "You work in a brothel and you don't want to have sex with me? We'll see about that."

As he grew closer toward Riley with his dick swinging at half-mast between his legs, she waited until he was within striking distance, then she kicked him as hard as she could with a snap-kick to his balls. The man doubled over in agony grasping his scrotum, then he reached behind him for his pistol, turning around to point it toward Riley. She glanced around looking for something to defend herself, noticing a broom in the corner. When she picked it up and swung the handle toward the man, he paused for a moment, laughing menacingly.

"You've got spunk, I'll give you that," he sniggered. "I'm going to enjoy taming this little filly."

As he advanced slowly toward her, Riley braced her feet the way Liza had taught her when they practiced sword-fighting, then she swung the handle rapidly downward, striking the man on his right wrist. His pistol tilted toward the floor, firing a loud round into the floorboards, and he reared up, preparing to strike her with his fist. Riley lunged forward, driving the tip of the broom into his solar plexus, then she struck him as hard as she could on the side of his temple.

When he crumpled unconscious onto the floor, an attractive middle-aged woman wearing a push-up corset opened the door, peering at the naked girl and the man lying on the floor with his bare ass pointing upward.

"Who the hell are you?" she said. "And what have you done to my best customer?"

R eady for more steamy chills and thrills? Order the next exciting volume in Riley's Time Travel Adventures:

In the outlaw frontier of the Wild West, you're either quick or you're dead...

ALSO BY VICTORIA RUSH

Wet your whistle a hundred different ways with Jade's Erotic Adventures. Browse the full collection of Victoria Rush steamy stories here:

Click to scan your favorites...

FOLLOW VICTORIA RUSH:

Want to keep informed of my latest erotic book releases? Sign up for my newsletter and receive a FREE bonus book:

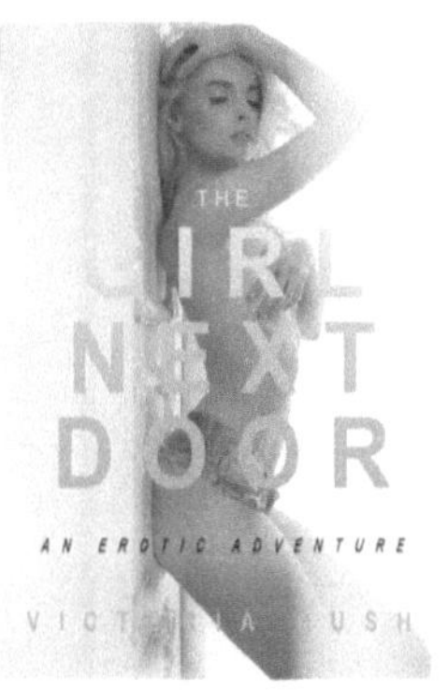

Spying on the neighbors just got a lot more interesting...